Alexander Morris

Nova Britannia

SALZWASSER
VERLAG

Alexander Morris

Nova Britannia

Reprint of the original.

1st Edition 2023 | ISBN: 978-3-37514-648-1

Verlag (Publisher): Salzwasser Verlag GmbH, Zeilweg 44, 60439 Frankfurt, Deutschland
Vertretungsberechtigt (Authorized to represent): E. Roepke, Zeilweg 44, 60439 Frankfurt, Deutschland
Druck (Print): Books on Demand GmbH, In de Tarpen 42, 22848 Norderstedt, Deutschland

NOVA BRITANNIA;

OR,

BRITISH NORTH AMERICA

ITS EXTENT AND FUTURE.

A LECTURE.

BY ALEXANDER MORRIS, A.M.,

ADVOCATE,

AUTHOR OF A PRIZE-ESSAY ON CANADA.

Published by Request of the Mercantile Library Association of Montreal

Montreal:
PRINTED BY JOHN LOVELL, AT THE CANADA DIRECTORY OFFICE,
ST. NICHOLAS STREET.

1858.

PREFACE.

In the course of the writer's own investigations as to the matters treated of in this Pamphlet, he felt the need of a brief Treatise, which should present a condensed bird's-eye view of British North America. With the intent of supplying that want, he compiled the facts here submitted as a Lecture. This he has now been induced, in compliance with a request to that effect, to publish, in the hope that the result of his inquiries may prove of some service in directing attention towards the important subject he treats of. In the historical, topographical, and descriptive portions of the Lecture, the writer has very freely used the statements of Andrews, in his excellent Report to the American Congress on the Trade of the British North American Colonies, and of Haliburton in his "History of Nova Scotia," without further acknowledgment than this general one. A list of other works made use of appears elsewhere. With these explanatory observations, the writer commits this pamphlet to the public, in the hope of leading his readers to appreciate more fully their position, as dwellers in a land of much promise, citizens of a country destined yet to assume the proportions of a great and powerful Britannic Northern Empire.

He moreover trusts, that, now when the prospect of a Union of the British American Colonies is engaging so much attention, this Lecture may prove of some slight service in urging on that desirable event.

MONTREAL, March, 1858.

The following Lecture was read before the Mercantile Library Association of Montreal, as part of its special course, on the 18th of March, 1858.

At the conclusion of the Lecture, the Honorable Peter McGill rose, and, addressing the President, stated that he had listened with much satisfaction to the lecture which had just been delivered. He believed its wide circulation would be productive of much good ; and he was sure he uttered the sentiments of every person present when he desired its publication. He would, therefore, move,

"That Mr. Morris be requested to publish the Lecture in pamphlet form, under the auspices of the Mercantile Library Association."

The Resolution was seconded by James Mitchell, Esq., and adopted by acclamation.

The President, T. S. Brown, Esq., then stated that the Association would be proud to secure for the Lecture wide publicity.

On the suggestion of W. Edmonstone, Esq., three cheers were given for the Queen, and the meeting closed.

NOVA BRITANNIA,

OR THE

BRITISH NORTH AMERICAN PROVINCES.

In acceding to the kind invitation of this Society to lecture before them, and thus complying with a practise which has become almost one of the institutions of the present age, I have preferred to select for this evening's consideration a subject of practical interest. It is impossible, within the brief limits of a fleeting hour, so to handle a large and comprehensive subject as its importance would merit; but my object will have been attained if by the instrumentality of this lecture any one is led to make the matter treated of the subject of his after reflection and inquiry. In fact, in this I believe the chief merit of the modern lecture to consist, that through it some topic of importance is treated in a popular style, and presented to the consideration of a general audience, in some of whom the spirit of inquiry may be enkindled, and thus they may be led onward and upward in the pursuit of knowledge and in the acquisition of general information.

Impressed, then, with this belief, I invite your attention for a brief space to a consideration of the present condition of the British North American Colonies; and shall, as I close, indulge in what some may deem the fanciful dream of an enthusiast, in regard to the future destiny of that immense tract of country, which extends from the Atlantic to in fact the Pacific coast, and which is now beginning, nay which already is making, rapid strides towards assuming that position, in the estimation of the European and American world, which its vast extent and its immense resources entitle it to. I believe that too few amongst us are by any means so familiar as we ought to be with the extent, capabilities, and actual position of the Lower Provinces, and the Island dependencies of Newfoundland and Prince Edward's Island. Their geographical position, their actual relations towards us, and the probability of their future closer alliance with Canada, give importance to such considerations, and justify me, a British American by birth, in to-

night, before this a Colonial audience, dealing
with questions deeply affecting the future of a
great Colonial empire. Providence has cast our
lot in a land destined to be a great country.
It cannot be time mis-spent to consider its present, to speculate as to its future, or even to imi-
tate the example of our good cousins across the
Lines and boast a little of our country, our
progress, and of our rapid advance in all that
constitutes the real greatness of a nation.

The subject is indeed an inviting one, thus to
trace from infancy the rise and progress of what
are now thickly populated Provinces; and many
suggestive thoughts crowd upon the mind as it
dwells upon the contemplation. Time will not
permit my entering upon many of these; but I
cannot refrain from a passing allusion to the
proud position which Britain holds in regard to
her Colonial empire. Strange, is it not, how
the mixed population of that, according to our
Cis-Atlantic ideas, little country, should have
so disseminated themselves and built up great
countries,—New Britains in all parts of the habi-
table globe. The triple cord which binds together the English, Irish, and Scotch into one
great people, who yet preserve to a considerable
extent their national characteristics, in support of
the British Constitution and of civil and religious

liberty, has given to Britain her immense power and her proud position. Swarms of her dense population have been drafted into the Old World and the New. Millions of people acknowledge her sway. Australia and British America, deriving from Britain their religion, their literature, their language, and their national characteristics, rival each other in the magnitude of their resources and in the rapidity of their development; and the impress of the British mind is stamped upon and reproduced, in what are in the lapse of time destined eventually to be great kindred nations, bound together by the ties of origin and by parental and filial affection. India, too, that great country towards which our sympathies are now so warmly turned,—that vast battle-field on which is even now going on the stern contest between light, civilization, and liberty,—the fierce fanaticism and blind hate of the proud Mussulman and the cringing but subtle and cruel Hindoo,—that great country in which the death-struggle of an effete and expiring religion is even now taking place, will still more and more be moulded by the influences of British energy and civilization, and will yet add a brilliant ornament to the crown which graces the temples of the Queen of Hindostan.

Aye, and on this continent a young but vigorous nation owes her origin and derives her national features from Old Britain, and, though to some extent temporarily alienated from the Parent State and obscured by internal discords and the dark blot of slavery, will yet, I doubt not, in the evolution of the world's history and the wondrous passing changes of events, be found, with India, Australia, and British America, combining with Britain in the defence of great constitutional principles, and in the maintenance of the world's liberty.

But I must revert from this passing allusion to the greatness of that Colonial empire of which we form a part, and which is rising up to national importance under the shade of the old flag, which, in the words of the poet, has "braved a thousand years the battle and the breeze," to the consideration of the British North American Colonial empire. And in dealing with the question, it shall be my aim to treat the subject popularly, avoiding statistics except when absolutely required in illustration or explanation.

Commencing, then, in geographical order, though not strictly so, I shall pass in brief review the Province of Nova Scotia and Cape Breton, the Labrador coast, and then the Islands of Newfoundland and Prince Edward. New Brunswick will next claim our notice; and passing on, the neglected Island of Anticosti,—as large, it may be observed, as Prince Edward's Island,—and our own Canada, will be considered. I shall then, pointing merely to that great undeveloped Northwest, to which the Ottawa valley is the natural highway, including the Red River country, the Saskatchewan Territory, New Caledonia, and Vancouver's Island, and, trusting that they will not stand aghast at the thought of such an infliction as an essay on so vast a subject, leave my readers to form their own impressions of the correctness of those hopes as to our future, which Colonists, whose all and whose destiny are here, are fain to cherish, as in the pride of their hearts they exclaim,

"This is my own, my native land!"

ACADIAN HISTORY.

The early history of Nova Scotia, from its discovery to its eventual final cession to the British at the treaty of Versailles, is a chequered and eventful one; but our time will not permit our tracing in detail the stirring history of Acadia. The early history of those discoveries which led to the settlement of British America may however be glanced at. To arrive at a tolerably correct outline of the result of those eventful discoveries, it will be well to consider, that, since Southern Oregon and Upper California have been absorbed into the United States, the continent of North America may be divided into four great sections, viz. :

The Russian Territory on the North-west,
The British Dominions on the North,
The United States in the centre,
And on the South, Mexico and Central America uniting with South America. " The most remarkable features of both North and South America are the rivers and the mountains, the former for their size and number, and the latter for their size and position, running in an unbroken chain from the northern to the southern extremity, having on the east side an immense breadth of country open to the rivers, four of which, the St. Lawrence, the Mississippi, the Amazon, and La Plata, are amongst the largest in the world, and but a narrow strip to the west, wider in the northern than the southern continent."

Such is the vast continent developed by the flood-tide of discovery, which, at the end of the 15th century, bore Columbus to the New World. In 1492, Columbus discovered, in the month of October, one of the Bahama Island; and afterwards the Continent. The success of the Spanish, stimulated the enterprise of the British, and in May, 1497, in the reign of Henry VII., John Cabot and his son Sebastian sailed from Bristol in the hope of finding a western passage to India. While pursuing a westerly course, in the hope of reaching the China seas, they saw land on the 24th of June. This they called Prima Vista, and it is believed to have been a part of Nova Scotia or Newfoundland. As Galvanus says that this land was in latitude 45°, it is ex-tremely probable that the expedition, in coasting, had entered the Gulf of St. Lawrence. During this part of their voyage they discovered an Island which they called St. John, now Prince Edward's Island. They then steered south to Florida. England therefore claimed America by disco-very and possession. The French next visited the continent. In 1518 and 1525, parties coasted along the shores from Newfoundland to Florida. In 1534, Jacques Cartier landed at Bay Chaleurs, and took possession in the name of the King of France. In 1579, an attempt was made by the British, under a charter from Queen Elizabeth, to colonize the Western World. The French follow-ed them in 1598, under De La Roche; but the early attempts were very calamitous, and the hold obtained upon the country was slight. In 1621, James I. granted all the country now Nova Scotia and New Brunswick, and Newfoundland,

to Sir William Alexander, afterwards Earl of
Stirling; and in 1628, Charles I. added another grant, *including Canada and the chief
part of the United States.* An order of Baronets was created, each of whom were to receive
16,000 acres of land, and who were to take seizin
on the Castle Hill of Edinburgh—Nova Scotia
being included in the county of that name. In
1629, Britain took possession of Cape Breton,
and held all this part of America; but attaching
little importance to it, Charles I., by the treaty
of St. Germains, in 1632, resigned to Louis XIII.
his right to New France. The progress of settlement went on. Cromwell reconquered Nova
Scotia, for the third time, in 1654; but in 1667
Charles II. relinquished Acadia to France.
Time went on, and, in 1710, New England conquered Nova Scotia, at an expense of £23,000,
by an expedition which sailed from Boston.
The treaty of Utrecht finally, in 1713, ensued,
and all Acadia or Nova Scotia was ceded to Great
Britain, and it has since so remained. New Brunswick was then included within its limits. In the
war of 1745, Cape Breton was conquered by the
Provincial troops. It was restored to France in
1749; but it again, in 1758, became the property of Britain. In 1759, the settlement proper
of Nova Scotia may be said to have commenced.

The subjugation of Prince Edward's Island took place in 1761. I pass by, as more familiar to my hearers, the early history, colonization, and settlement of Canada; merely remarking, that by the treaty of Versailles, at Paris in 1763, France resigned all her claims in North America to Britain.

Such, then, is a compressed outline of the leading events in the earlier European history of this portion of British North America; and it is now time to glance at the position of Nova Scotia and the other Provinces, which were once so undervalued, that on Champlain's return to France he found the minds of people divided with regard even to Canada, some thinking it not worth possessing.

NOVA SCOTIA.

The Province of Nova Scotia now includes Cape Breton, from which it is severed by the Straits of Canso. Nova Scotia proper, says Andrews, is a long peninsula nearly wedge-shaped, connected at its eastern and broadest extremity with the continent of America by an isthmus only 15 miles wide. This narrow slip of land separates the waters of the Bay of Fundy from those of the Gulf of St. Lawrence. The peninsula, 280 miles in length, fronts the Atlantic ocean.

The Island of Cape Breton is a singularly formed network of streams and lakes, and it is

separated into two parts, with the exception of
an isthmus but 767 yards wide, by the Bras
d'Or Lake, an arm of the sea. The most remarkable feature in the peninsula of Nova Scotia is
the numerous indentations along its coasts. A
vast and uninterrupted body of water, impelled
by the trade-wind from the coast of Africa to the
American continent, forms a current along the
coast till it strikes the Nova Scotian shore
with great force, and rolls its tremendous
tides, of 60 or 70 feet in height, up the Bay
of Fundy, which bounds Nova Scotia on the
north-west. The harbours of Nova Scotia on
its Atlantic coast are unparalleled in the world.
Between Halifax and Cape Canso there are 12
ports capable of receiving ships of the line, and
14 others of sufficient depth for merchantmen.
The peninsula of Nova Scotia is supposed to contain 9,534,196 acres, and, including Cape Breton, 12,000,000. The country is undulating,
and abounds with lakes. The scenery is pictu-
resque. Nova Scotia is possessed, it is believed,
of valuable mineral wealth, including large fields
of coal. The development of these riches has
however been checked by the fact, that in the
year 1826 a charter was granted to the Duke of
York, for the term of 60 years, of the mines and
minerals of the Province. The lease was assign-

ed to an English Company, which now holds it. The Province has recently come to an arrangement with this company, by which they are confined within certain limits. Still, in 1849, 208,000 chaldrons were shipped to the States. The other minerals which are turned to economic uses, are iron, manganese, gypsum, &c.

The western and milder section of Nova Scotia is distinguished for its productiveness in fruits. Wheat grows well in the eastern and in the central parts of Nova Scotia. In 1851, 297,157 bushels were raised, of which 186,497 were grown in Sydney, Pictou, Colchester, and Cumberland, a fact which shows the superiority of that section of the Province for the growth of wheat,—a peculiarity which extends along the whole north-eastern shore of New Brunswick to the boundary of Canada. Oats, hay, peas, beans, potatoes, turnips, &c. are raised in large quantities, and butter and cheese are made freely. The character of Nova Scotia for farm stock is good. My hearers may be surprised to learn that Nova Scotia exceeds 14 wheat-growing States and Territories of the Union in the growth of wheat and barley; and all the States and Territories in oats, buckwheat, potatoes, hay, butter. The trade of Nova Scotia is large. In 1850 its imports were 5 millions of dollars, and its exports

3 millions. In its general and fishing trade it employs a large marine, which must prove a fruitful nursery for seamen. In 1851 there were 3228 vessels entered inwards, 3265 outwards. In 1851 Nova Scotia had a fishing fleet of 812 vessels, manned by 3681 men, and the number of boats engaged was 5161. The total value of its fisheries for 1851 exceeded a million of dollars. The population of the Province was at last census, in that year, 276,117 souls. There were in 1851, 1096 schools and 31,354 scholars. Nova Scotia has reclaimed by dykes 40,012 acres of land. Cape Breton too has a large trade, produces large quantities of fish, and there is mined besides a considerable amount of coal.

NEWFOUNDLAND

Lies on the north-east side of the entrance to the St. Lawrence, separated from Canada by the Gulf. Its south-west point approaches Cape Breton within about 46 miles, the Straits of Belle Isle to the north and northwest separate it from the shores of Labrador, the Atlantic washes it on the east. It is triangular in form, broken by bays, creeks, and estuaries. Its circuit is 1000 miles. Its breadth at the widest is 300 miles, its extreme length 419. From the sea it has a wild, sterile appearance. It is rugged in character, hills and valleys succeeding each other. It comprises woods, marshes, and barrens; the woods clothing the sides and summits of the hills, and the valleys and low lands. The trees are pine, spruce, fir, larch, and birch. Recently in the survey of the Atlantic Telegraph, pine of most excellent quality was found in the interior of the island. The marshes are not necessarily low or level land, but are often undulated and elevated a considerable height above the sea. They are open tracts covered with moss. The barrens are exposed elevated tracts, covered with scanty vegetation. The most remarkable general feature of the country is the great abundance of lakes, which are found even on the tops of the hills. In fact, it is estimated that one third of the surface of the whole island is covered with fresh-water. The area is 23,040,000 acres. Fishing has employed the population chiefly, and not over 200,000 acres are under cultivation. The climate too is variable, its vicissitudes being great. Spring comes on more slowly than in Canada. Summer is shorter, and the winter a series of storms, winds, rain, and snow. The last rarely remains long on the ground, and the frost is never so intense as in Western Canada. This arises no doubt from its

insular position. The population in 1852 was
125,000, of whom 30,000 were directly engaged
in the fisheries. In 1845, 9900 boats were
engaged in the fisheries. The annual value
of the produce of the colony has been estimated
at $6,000,000, and the value of the property
engaged in the fisheries at $2,500,000. The ex-
ports in 1851 were $4,801,000, employing 1013
vessels. The imports were $4,455,180. New-
foundland exported in that year, to Spain,
Portugal, Italy, and the Brazils, to the extent of
$1,500,000. The fisheries carried on are cod,
the great staple, and the herring, mackerel, salmon, whale, and seal fisheries.

The principal town of Newfoundland is St.
John. It is alleged that a fast steamer could
cross from thence to Galway in five days. It is
distant from Ireland but 1665 miles. Its geographical position is very important, and its fisheries are a source of inexhaustible wealth. It
carries on a large foreign trade, inclusively of an
extensive one with the West Indies.

LABRADOR.

Of the Labrador coast little is known. It
was at one time included in Canada, but was re-
annexed to Newfoundland in 1808. It has a sea-
coast of over 100 miles, and is frequented during

summer by 20,000 persons. This vast country, equal in extent to France, Spain, and Germany, has a resident population of 9000 souls, including the Esquimaux and the Moravians. The climate is very severe, but the sea on its shores teems with wealth. Seals and salmon are very plentiful. The furs are very valuable. The exports from this coast are cod, herring, salmon, sealskins, cod and seal oil, furs, and feathers. Andrews, from the best data at his command, states that the exports from this coast are of the annual value of $2,784,000; but they are by some estimated as high as $4,000,000. Its imports are $600,000 per annum.

PRINCE EDWARD'S ISLAND.

I now glance at Prince Edward's Island, which is situated in a deep recess on the western side of the Gulf of St. Lawrence. It is separated from New Brunswick and Nova Scotia by the Straits of Northumberland, which at the narrowest are only 9 miles wide. The island is crescent-shaped, 130 miles in length, and at its greater breadth 34 miles. The east point is 27 miles from Cape Breton, and 125 miles from Cape Ray, Newfoundland. It is a level country, well adapted for agricultural purposes. Wheat, oats, and barley are the staple products. Its area is 2134

square miles. In 1848 the population was
62,678. The climate is neither so cold in winter
nor so hot in summer as in Lower Canada. One
drawback to the progress of the island has been
the holding of the land by non-resident land-
lords, who lease the soil. From the productiveness and the other advantages of the soil,
it might, says Monro, easily sustain 1,000,000
persons. There are 231 schools in the island,
supported by a tax on real estate, and attended
by 9922 pupils. The exports in 1854 were
$596,608. In 1851, 621 ships were entered
inwards, and 621 outwards. The island is believed to have been discovered by Cabot in 1497.
In 1761 it became permanently a territory of
Great Britain.

NEW BRUNSWICK.

I now turn to New Brunswick, which abuts
Canada. In 1784 it was erected into a Province distinct from Nova Scotia. Its length
is 190 miles, its breadth 150. It lies nearly
in the form of a rectangle, and is bounded on
the south-east by the Bay of Fundy and Nova
Scotia, on the west by Maine, on the north-
west by Canada and the Bay of Chaleurs, on the
east by Northumberland Straits and the Gulf of
St. Lawrence. It contains 32,000 square miles

or 22,000,000 of acres, and a population of 210,000 inhabitants. It has a sea-coast of 400 miles, with many harbours. Its staple trades are shipbuilding, the fisheries, and the timber trade. Its great agricultural capabilities are only now beginning to be known. The Commissioners appointed by the Imperial Government to survey the line for the proposed railway from Halifax to Quebec, thus speak of New Brunswick in their report, and their testimony is a weighty one:—

"Of the climate, soil, and capabilities of New Brunswick it is impossible to speak too highly. There is not a country in the world so beautifully wooded and watered. An inspection of the map will show that there is scarcely a section of it without its streams, from the running brook up to the navigable river. Two thirds of its boundary are washed by the sea; the remainder is embraced by the large rivers the St. John and the Restigouche. The beauty and richness of scenery of this latter river and its branches, are rarely surpassed by anything on this continent.

"The lakes of New Brunswick are numerous and most beautiful; its surface is undulating, hill and dale varying up to mountain and valley. It is everywhere, except a few peaks of the highest mountains, covered with dense forests of the finest growth.

"The country can everywhere be penetrated by its streams. In some parts of the interior, a canoe, by a portage of three or four miles only, can float away either to the Bay of Chaleurs or the Gulf of St. Lawrence, or down to St. John and the Bay of Fundy. Its agricultural capabilities and climate are described by Bouchette, Martin, and other authors. The country is by them, and most deservedly so, highly praised. For any great plan of emigration, or colonization, there is not another British colony which presents such a favorable field as New Brunswick.

"On the surface is an abundant stock of the finest timber, which in the markets of England realizes large sums annually, and affords an unlimited supply to the settler. If the forests should ever become exhausted, there are the coal-fields beneath. The rivers, lakes, and sea-coast abound with fish."

Such is the sister Province of New Brunswick; and though I am assured, on undoubted personal authority, that a large extent of her very best agricultural territory reaching onwards to Canada is still a primeval forest, still her position in regard to her trade relations is no insignificant one, as will appear from the following statements.

The total imports of New Brunswick in 1851 were $4,852,440, and the exports $3,780,105. There were 3058 ships entered inwards, and 2981 outwards. The fisheries of New Brunswick are valuable, and those in the Bay of Fundy in 1850 realized $263,500. The timber floated down the St. John is very large; the quantity was estimated in 1852 at $1,945,000. There is room in New Brunswick for a large population. In 1855 there were only 6,000,000 acres of land granted, and of these but 700,000 were under cultivation. 11,000,000 acres of land continued ungranted. As to agricultural capabilities, New Brunswick—strange as the tale may seem— exceeds in wheat 14 wheat-growing States of the Union, and in barley 24 out of 30; in oats, buckwheat, and potatoes, 30 States and Territories; and in butter and hay, all the States. In the growth of potatoes, hay, and oats, Munro asserts that no State in the Union can compete with New Brunswick, whether as regards weight, quality, or quantity. The average produce per Imperial acre of wheat is 19 bushels, of barley 28, oats 34, and of potatoes 226, and turnips 456; outstripping New York, Ohio, and Canada West in these. The value of the agricultural products of New Brunswick, exclusive of farm-stock, was estimated in 1854 at £2,000,000. There were in 1851, 798 schools, attended by 18,892 children, and in 1853, 24,127. Professor Johnston estimated that the agricultural resources alone of New Brunswick would enable it to sustain a population of $5\frac{1}{2}$ millions. The climate is similar to our own. The coal-field of New Brunswick is very extensive: its area has been estimated by Gesner at 10,000 square miles. The earlier history of New Brunswick is embraced in that of Nova Scotia, and need not here be particularly referred to.

With regard to the position of the Acadian Provinces, and their relations towards the other portions of British America, and the community of interest which is arising, I avail myself of the judicious statements of Principal Dawson of McGill College, Montreal, in a lecture delivered before the Natural History Society of Montreal, on the Acadian Provinces :—

"Their progress in population and wealth is slow, in comparison with that of Western America, though equal to the average of that of the American Union, and more rapid than that of the older States. Their agriculture is rapidly improving, manufacturing and mining enterprises are extending themselves, and railways are being built to connect them with the more inland parts of the continent. Like Great Britain, they possess important minerals in which the neighbouring parts of the continent are deficient, and enjoy the utmost facilities for commercial pursuits. Ultimately, therefore, they must have with the United States, Canada, and the fur countries, the same commercial relations that Britain maintains with western, central, and northern Europe. Above all, they form the great natural oceanic termination of the great valley of the St. Lawrence; and although its commerce has hitherto, by the skill and industry of its neighbours, been drawn across the natural barrier which Providence has placed between it and the sea-ports of the United States, it must ultimately take its natural channel; and then not only will the cities on the St. Lawrence be united by the strongest common interests, but they will be bound to Acadia by ties more close than any merely political union. The great thoroughfares to the rich lands and noble scenery of the West, and thence to the sea-breezes and salt-water of the Atlantic, and to the great seats of industry and art in the old world, will pass along the St. Lawrence, and through the Lower Provinces. The surplus agricultural produce of Canada will find its nearest consumers among the miners, shipwrights, mariners, and fishermen of Acadia; and they will send back the treasures of their mines and of their sea. This ultimate fusion of all the populations extending along this great river, valley, and estuary, and the establishment throughout its course of one of the principal streams of American commerce, seems in the nature of things inevitable; and there is already a large field for the profitable employment of laborers and capital in accelerating this desirable result."

Giving due attention to these sound and cautious views of a writer thoroughly acquainted with his subject, and himself an Acadian, which meet an objection often raised as to the presumed absence of any common objects or community of interest between the Acadian Provinces and Canada, we now advance towards that Province, and find, to the northward of Prince Edward's Island, the Magdalen Islands, under the jurisdiction of Canada, and for electoral purposes included in the County of Gaspé. They are 7 in number, and are used as fishing stations. Their population in 1851 was 2500. These islands are almost in the centre of the Gulf of St. Lawrence, and the length of the group is 56 miles. They are owned by Captain Coffin in strict entail. The value of the exports of the fisheries was in 1848, $224,000.

Within the Gulf, and at the very threshold of Canada, is the large Island of Anticosti, 420 miles below Quebec. It comprises 2,000,000 of acres. It has been till lately owned in England, but has been much neglected. The recent Geological Survey under the direction of Sir William Logan will serve to dispel many existing prejudices. It is believed to contain much arable land, and it is well wooded. It should be no longer overlooked, as its position is very important, and it may become an important *entrepôt* of trade.

CANADA.

And now we have arrived at our own fair Canada, and I shall not weary you with a long detail of dry and dull figures: you can find those elsewhere. But the mind naturally dwells with pleasure on the contemplation of the rapid rise, steady growth, present prosperity, and brilliant future of this our country. Canada, with her population of 2,500,000, her steady flow of emigration, her rising manufactures, her mineral wealth, her agricultural advantages, her magnificent system of inland navigation afforded by her canals and her new Mediterranean, her great railway (the longest in the world), her highway to Europe, and her successful ocean-line of steamers, is bounding on with fresh vigour, and steadily assuming the proportions of a great and prosperous people. Canada is no longer looked upon as a dismal, dreary waste of snow-clad hills. Our representations at the Universal Exhibitions have dispelled many a prejudice, and the people of Europe and of Britain have learned to regard our country as a home, where, free from the keener competition of the Old World, and sheltered under the protecting power of Britain, men can work their way to independence and comfort, and see their families taking positions of respectability around them.

Here we have scope and verge enough: our population of 2,500,000 has an extent about six times that of England and Wales for its expansion, no less than 346,863 square miles; and very surely and steadily is our population augmenting, eclipsing in its progress that of the United States. How rapid that increase has been will appear on the most impartial testimony, from the following extract, from *Hunt's Merchants' Magazine* for February last:—

"When it is remembered that in 1848 the population of United Canada was about 1,500,000, the rate of increase in ten years is indeed something to boast of. Two thirds added to the population of a country with such variety of soil and climate, in that time, is without precedent. The increase of the United States during the ten years ending 1850 was 35½ per cent., that of Upper Canada during the 10 years from 1841 to 1851, 104½ per cent., and now for the whole Province, since 1848, it is 65 to 70 per cent, or nearly double the rate of increase of the United States. The third of a century is generally reckoned as a generation. During that period the population of Canada has increased from 582,000 to 2,500,000, or more than twice doubled itself. If that rate be continued, Canada will have at the beginning of the next century 20,000,000 of inhabitants."

And then as an outlet for our population, and a legitimate field for the development of the energies of our people, beyond us lies that great stretch of territory, of which the newly chosen Seat of Government holds the key, the Ottawa Valley, with its 80,000 square miles of country, through which the Atlantic and Pacific Railway will yet take its course, and the products of the great Western States seek the seaboard when the Ottawa navigation shall have been improved.

RUPERT'S LAND.

And then above us again is that vast expanse, claimed by the Hudson's Bay adventurers, which will yet, and it may be soon, be inhabited by a large population, comprising as it does, 3,060,000 square miles.

This great country cannot much longer remain unoccupied; and if we do not proceed to settle it, the Americans will appropriate it, as they did Oregon, and the Mormons are said to be threatening New Caledonia. Without entering into the question of the alleged vices in the charter by which that powerful company holds its possessions, and the mode of adjudicating thereon, there are certain practical measures which should be at once adopted. A means of communication by road and water, for summer and winter use, should be opened between Lake Superior and the Red River Settlement, and that forthwith; and that Settlement should, as of right belonging to it, be placed under the jurisdiction of Canada, with power to this Province to colonize the territory. This power should at once be given, and will doubtless be conceded on the application of Ca-

nada. This obtained, and a settlement of 7,000
souls added to our population as a centre of
operations, steps can be taken for obtaining more
accurate information as to the nature of the immense tract of territory, of which a large part
once belonged to the 100 partners of Old France,
and, though believed to be the property of Canada, is now held by the Hudson's Bay Company.
The great valley of the Saskatchewan should
form the subject of immediate attention. Enough
is known to satisfy us, that, though in the northerly portions of that territory commonly known
as the Hudson's Bay Territory a Siberian climate
prevails, yet there is a vast region well adapted
for becoming the residence of a large population.
Once the Red River Settlement is opened to our
commerce, a wide field extends before our enterprise ; and those who recollect or have other-
wise become familiar with the struggles, 40 years
ago, of even the settlers in Western Canada, and
the painful, toilsome warfare with which they
conquered that rising portion of the Province
from the wilderness, will regard the task of colonization as a comparatively light one.

The press has for some time been teeming
with articles on the subject of this Territory,
and has done good service thereby, and, though
there is not opportunity here to enter upon

the subject at length, yet, while not going so far as those who would paint all that Territory—some of it bleak and inhospitable enough —as a paradise, I hesitate not to assert, that there are many millions of acres richly arable and possessed of a climate milder than our own. In proof of this position I will say a word or two as to the Red River country, in which Lord Selkirk's settlement was planted, taking, as recent and reliable authorities the Rev. Jno. Ryerson, 1855, and Bond's Minnesota. The Red River Settlement is 700 miles distant from Fort William, on Lake Superior, by the travelled way, but a route of 456 miles can be opened. The Red River rises in Minnesota, and, running northward, discharges into Lake Winnipeg. It is navigable for boats for 150 miles from its mouth. The Assiniboia River rises west of the Red River, and forms a junction with it 55 miles from the mouth of the latter. The English and Scotch settlers extend along both sides of Red River from the Assiniboia to Lower Fort Garry, 20 miles below. This is far the best post of the settlement. 18 windmills are scattered along the west bank, upon which this lengthy serpentine village is principally situated.

Sir George Simpson, in his Overland Journey, says :—

" The soil of the Red River is a black mould of considerable depth, which, when first tilled, produces extraordinary crops,—as much, on some occasions, as 40 returns of wheat,—and even after 20 successive years of cultivation, without the relief of manure or of fallow or of green crop, it still yields from 15 to 25 bushels per acre. The wheat produced is plump and heavy. There are also large quantities of grain of all kinds, besides beef, mutton, pork, butter, cheese and wool, in abundance."

As to the character of this settlement, Ryerson also says :—

" The soil is of black mould, and the settlement yields good crops of wheat, barley, oats, pease, and potatoes. The spacious prairies afford pasture in the open season, and furnish abundance of hay for the winter. Over the boundless pastures roam thousands of sheep, black cattle, and horses. There is however no export trade in the Colony. The Hudson's Bay Company pay for what they wish to consume, and thus afford the only market. The wheat is ground by windmills. There are no sawmills, fulling-mills, or factories of any kind. A large portion of the settlers are hunters, and the number of buffaloes in the Hudson's Bay Territory is immense. The settlers have many difficulties to contend with."

Hear again another authority (whose zealous discharge of his duties led him to visit Prince Rupert's Land) as to the Red River Settlement.

The former Bishop of Montreal, and now of Quebec, in 1844, said :—

" The soil, which is alluvial, is beyond example rich and productive, and withal so easily worked, that, although it does not quite come up to the description of the Happy Islands, *reddit ubi cererem tellus inarata quot annos*, there is an instance, I was assured, of a farm in which the owner, with comparatively light labour in the preparatory processes, had taken a wheat crop out

of the same land for 18 successive years, never changing the crop,
never manuring the land, and never suffering it to lie fallow, and
that the crop was abundant to the last; and with respect to the
pasture and hay, they are to be had *ad libitum*, as nature gives
them in the open plains.

These testimonies have lately received the
most entire corroboration. Professor Hind, in
his Report to the Canadian Government of his
visit there, in the summer of last year, fully con-
firms all these statements.

He describes the valley of the Red River, and
a large portion of the country on its affluent, as
a " paradise of fertility." He finds it " impossible
to speak of it in any other terms than those
which may express astonishment and admiration."
He states that " the character of the soil cannot
be surpassed, and that all kinds of farm produce
common in Canada succeed admirably in the
District of the Assiniboia"; and he declares em-
phatically, " that as an agricultural country it
will one day rank among the most distinguished."

Such, then, is that little colony composed of
Scottish Highlanders and their descendants, and
of French Canadians, which is even now a peti-
tioner at the portals of our Legislature for ad-
mission to those inherent rights of free and self
government which every Briton inherits as a
birth-right, and which the statesmen of Britain
have learned—and I doubt not Canadian poli-

ticians have had their share in the inculcation of
the lesson—to concede to British subjects in all
territories under the sway of the Royal Sceptre.
Colonial Government has in our days assumed a
new phase. It must, to continental eyes, have
been a strange spectacle, as it was in our view a
noble one, that was presented, when the assent
of the little Colony of Newfoundland was required
to give validity to a solemn treaty agreed to
between two of the mightiest of European nations;
and stranger still, to see that little colony resolute-
ly vetoing the arrangement. This result must have
grated harshly on the feelings of Imperial Military France. But it should be viewed by colonists
as a convincing proof of the readiness of the
Parent State to act justly by her Colonial children ; and with such a precedent before us, can we
doubt as to whether the rights of these Red
River colonists will be protected, if properly urged
and sustained by Canada.

Imperial interests, as well as Colonial ur-
gently demand the opening up of that vast stretch
of rich agricultural territory of which the Red
River " holds the key." Apart from the arable
areas on the highway between Canada and the
Red River, that settlement forms a nucleus
round which will gather a dense population
scattered over those vast prairies, covered with the

rankest luxuriance of vegetation, and holding
out to settlers the rich inducements of 1,300,000
acres of arable land and 3,000,000 acres of grazing
country. Should such a "paradise of fertility" as
this remain longer locked up ? Will the gather-
ing of a few peltries compensate for the with-
drawal of such a region from the industry of our
race ? Assuredly not. The knell of arbitrary rule
has been rung. The day has gone by for the per-
petuation of monopolies. The Baronets of Nova
Scotia would fare but ill in our times, unless moral
worth accompanied their rank. Provinces are
not so lightly shared and parcelled as they once
were. As for our own Province, self-government
has been conceded to us, and the largest measure
of political liberty is enjoyed by our people. We
are left to carve out our own destiny; and I
shrewdly suspect that few among us will regard
with much admiration that ancient and vener-
able parchment, which, under the sign-manual
of Charles II., by the Grace of God, King of
'England, Scotland, France, and Ireland, recites
that he, " being desirous to promote all endea-
vours tending to the public good of our people,
have of our especial grace, certain knowledge,
and mere motion given, granted, ratified, and
confirmed unto our entirely beloved cousin
Prince Rupert, the Duke of Albemarle, *et al.*, by the

name of the Governor and Company of Adventurers of England, trading into Hudson's Bay, the sole trade and commerce of all those seas, streights, bays, rivers, lakes, creeks, and sounds, in whatsoever latitude they shall lie, within the entrance of the streights commonly called Hudson's Streights; together with all the lands and territories upon the countries, coasts, and confines of the seas, bays, lakes, rivers, creeks, and sounds aforesaid, that are not already actually possessed by the subjects of any other Christian Prince or State, with the fishing of all sorts of fish, whales, sturgeons, and all other royal fishes in the seas, bays, islets, and rivers within the premises, and the fish therein taken, together with the royalty of the sea upon the coasts within the limits aforesaid, and all mines royal, as well discovered as not discovered, of gold, silver, gems, and precious stones, to be found or discovered within the territories aforesaid." And what think you is the price which this charter provides shall be paid for this munificent, this princely gift,—of, as the Hudson's Bay Company view it, half a continent,—for this comprehensive donation of everything, but the sky, which overhangs Prince Rupert's Land. Ah, here it is, and very onerous and burdensome this same company of adventurers must have found their vassalage to be: "yielding and paying," saith this grave title-deed, with which the onward rush of settlement is attempted to be stayed, somewhat, it must be confessed, after the fashion of the celebrated Mrs. Partington, when mop in hand she valiantly endeavoured to sweep out the incursion of the angry Atlantic,—"yielding and paying to us, our heirs and successors, for the same, two elks and two black beavers"—not yearly, mark you, but magnanimously—"whensoever and as often as we, our heirs and successors, shall happen to enter into the said countries, territories, and regions hereby granted"; and then, by all sorts of right lawyerly phrases, not only "the whole, entire, and only trade and traffic and use and privilege of trading is granted, but also the whole trade to and with all the natives and people inhabiting, or which *shall inhabit*, within the territories, lands, and coasts aforesaid"; and all sorts of pains and penalties are threatened against all those who do visit, haunt, frequent, or trade, traffic or adventure into the said countries; and all such shall, saith the Royal Charles, "incur our Royal indignation, and the forfeiture and loss of the goods and merchandize so brought." But time does not permit the dwelling longer on this relic of antiquity. It will suffice to express my confident belief, that Canada has only to express in firm but respectful tones her demands as to that vast territory, and these will be cheerfully acceded to by Britain. Those demands should be ripely considered, and so matured as to evince, not a mere grasping thirst of territorial aggrandizement, but a large-spirited and comprehensive appreciation of the requirements of the country, and a proper sense of the responsibilities to be assumed in regard to the well-being of the native and other inhabitants, and the due developement of the resources of the territory. In such a spirit our statesmen will I trust be found acting. The position of our Province too is to be weighed. To a large portion of the Territory we have an indubitable legal claim; to another portion the Crown of Britain would be entitled: but all that is adapted for settlement should be placed under the jurisdiction of representative government, and any further extension of the rights of the Company to trade in the more northerly regions should be subjected to the approval or control of Colonial authorities. The subject is not without its difficulties; but, I doubt not, these can all be satisfactorily overcome; and the interests of the whole Empire imperiously demand their prompt and satisfactory adjustment.

VANCOUVER'S ISLAND.

But now, to hasten on to the end of this our long journey, and, traversing the country stretching towards the Pacific, you will find the climate gradually becoming milder as we approach the ocean. And we have at length reached the Pacific, and Vancouver's Island, a British possession, improvidently leased to the Hudson's Bay Company, but whose lease will expire in 1859, and which is now, it appears, to be committed to a military government. "This splendid island," says Nicolay, "is in form long and narrow; in length about 250 miles, in average breath 50; with a surface of upwards of 12,000 square miles. A range of lofty hills extends through its whole length; and it is perhaps even more fertile, and has more open glades and land fit for cultivation than the Southern Continental shore. Its western side is pierced by deep canals, and it has many excellent harbours. It has beautiful rivers of water; and clumps and groves of trees are scattered through the level lands. The Hudson's Bay Company have here established a large cattle farm and post called Victoria. At the northern extremity of the island there is a large and excellent field of coal." Iron, copper, and silver, according to Spanish writers, are found there; and gold, according to more recent accounts. Martin, the apologist of the Hudson's Bay Company's regime, testifies to the excellence of the climate of the island, and to its adaptation for the cultivation of wheat and other grains; and further states, that,—

"The position, resources, and climate of Vancouver's Island eminently adapt it for being the Britain of the Northern Pacific. There is no port between the Straits of Juan de Fuco and San Francisco; it is within a week's sail of California; within double that distance from the Sandwich Islands, with which a thriving trade has already been established; five days' voyage from Sitka or New Archangel, the head-quarters of the Russian Fur Company's settlements, where large supplies of provisions are required, and it is within three weeks' steaming distance of Japan. This commanding position justifies the expectation that Vancouver's Island will become, not only a valuable agricultural settlement, but also a rich commercial *entrepot* for British trade and industry."

He also adds, that " whether it be possible to establish regular and rapid communication, *via* Canada, with the coast of the Pacific, remains to be ascertained"; and concludes with the remark, that " by whatever means Vancouver's Island be brought within half its present distance of England, great good cannot fail to accrue to the Colony and to the Parent State." That desirable result is, I trust, not very far distant, and I elsewhere point out the mode of its attainment.

GENERAL RESULTS.

And now, my hearers, we have travelled in company from the Atlantic to the Pacific. What think you of your journey, and of those Britannic possessions in which your lot is cast? Is there not here the germ of a mighty people? Are not these Colonies a fitting appanage to the great Empire under whose protection they are being developed? Will they not be, nay I would say are they not *now*, a brilliant jewel in the crown of our beloved and gracious Sovereign Queen Victoria, who so worthily graces her throne?

For bring together the gross results of our investigations, and what do we find?

1stly. That the Maritime Provinces alone comprise 86,000 square miles, and, as we may safely assume, are capable of sustaining a population nearly as great as England,—their natural productions and resources being very similar in kind and amount. They are as large as Holland, Greece, Belgium, Portugal, and Switzerland, all put together. New Brunswick alone is as large as the Kingdom of Sardinia, and Nova Scotia is larger than Switzerland.

2ndly. We have Canada, with her 346,863 square miles of territory, with her great Lakes,—

which alone comprise an extent of space equa to that of Britain and Wales, and larger in volume than the Caspian Sea,—and her railways, canals, agricultural capabilities, rising manufactures, and enterprising people.

And 3rdly. We have the North-west Territory of British America, with, according to Arrowsmith," its 3,060,000 square miles of country, extending from the Pacific Ocean and Vancouver's Island along the parallel of 49' north latitude, near the head of Lake Superior, and thence in an easterly direction to the coast of Labrador and the Atlantic." Place all this in one view, and we find that we can endorse the views of the Hon. Joseph Howe, when he exclaimed in the Nova Scotian House of Assembly.—

"Beneath, around, and behind us, stretching away from the Atlantic to the Pacific, are 4,000,000 square miles of territory. All Europe with its family of nations contains but 3,708,000, or 292,000 miles less. The United States includes 3,300,572 square miles, or 769,128 less than British America. Sir, I often smile when I hear some vain-glorious Republican exclaiming,

'No pent-up Utica contracts our powers :
The whole unbounded continent is ours !'

forgetting that the largest portion does not belong to him at all, but to us the men of the North, whose descendants will control its destinies forever. The whole globe contains but 37,000,000 square miles. We North Americans under the British flag have one ninth of the whole, and this ought to give us ample room and verge enough for the accommodation and support of a countless population."

Then grouping our population, we have, in the organized Provinces, three millions of people, at the lowest computation.

Combining our trade returns, we had in 1851 exports to the extent of 25 millions of dollars, and a revenue of £1,153,979 8s. 3d.; but it is now much larger. The revenue of Canada alone in 1856, was £1,238,666; and then, as nations now-a-days need a safety-valve, like the national debt of England, we too in 1851 had a national debt of £4,691,509, but of which Canada bears the lion's share. In 1856 the direct liability of Canada, incurred for public improvements, was £4,703,303.

FUTURE PROSPECTS.

If we pass in review the advantages of all these Provinces, the agricultural resources of Canada, its manufacturing capabilities, its mineral wealth, its rising trade, its great means of water communication, its systems of railways, the vast stretch of undeveloped country beyond us; and then the agricultural resources and capabilities of New Brunswick, and its maritime facilities; the commanding position of Nova Scotia, its coal-fields and extensive fisheries; the mind is most favorably impressed with the magnitude of their combined resources. And to all this when we bring

before us the fleet of the maritime Provinces, and
the hosts of sturdy colonists who man them, and
consider the energetic character inherited by our
people, which the fusion of races, and · the
conquering from the forest of new territories, has
fostered, and the influences of our climate have
rendered hardier ;—who, considering our present
and looking back upon our past, can doubt but
that a great future is before these Colonies.
Nay, is it not manifest that the day must come
when they will play no mean part in the world's
history and amid the ranks of nations.

That this is no rash assertion, the history of
other nations will justify us in assuming. Let
us for instance take our parent Britain as an
example, and who could have foretold the future
of that island people. How wondrous her rise,
how vast her influence throughout the world, giving her sons a right to claim a position analogous
to that of the citizen of another empire of the
olden time, as he pronounced the magic words,
"I am a Roman citizen!" and yet, as we look
back over history, how humble her origin. Rising in population by almost imperceptible increase, Froud says, that, at the time of the
Spanish Armada, a rough census then taken
gave a population to England of only about five
millions. How vast its increase since then ! and

why, with all that modern civilisation is doing for
us, should not British America follow in the foot-
steps of her parent ?

Surely it is a noble destiny that is before
us ; and who, as he reflects upon all these things,
does not feel an honest pride as he thinks that
he too may, in however humble a sphere, or by
however feeble an effort, aid in urging on that
great destiny. It is not my purpose to trench upon
the political in this lecture, nor would it be con-
sistent with the purposes of your Society that I
should thus interfere with any of those questions
of the day which, in one shape or other, are press-
ing upon the consideration of us all; yet in
dwelling upon the present and the future of these
Provinces, it is impossible to avoid glancing at the
question of how that future will be shaped. One
of two events, it has been said, are in the course
of time likely to occur; namely, that either those
Provinces will form a combination with the
American Union, or with a portion of it,—a pos-
sibility that I believe to be altogether and in every
way undesirable,—or, what I am sure this audience would infinitely prefer, that they will stand
together, a great Britannic Confederation, thoroughly imbued with the true principles of liberty,
and reflecting the character of that great parent
country from which their inhabitants have mainly

sprung, and rising to power and strength under her
guiding influence. Let me not be misunderstood:
I do not say that such an event as even this last
contingency is an immediately impending one;
but I do say, that, in the natural course of events,
such changes will come, as surely as the child
becomes the man, or the feeble sapling becomes
the sturdy monarch of the forest. That day may
be, and I trust is, far distant; but sure I am that
whatever, in the upheavings of the Old World
and the restless whirl of events, may betide, yet
the connection between our country and the Parent
State will not be rudely severed, but fostered by
the power and might of Britain, and, rising in
strength and power, thousands of strong hands
and bold hearts within our borders will cherish
towards Britain sentiments of warm affection and
attached loyalty, and will be ready, if need be, in
the contests for liberty that may arise, to stand
side by side in the foremost rank with the armies
of Britain.

There is, indeed, vast room for speculation as
to the future of this great British Colonial Empire, and its consideration has engrossed and is
engrossing the energies of many minds. Amongst
others, hear what Senator Seward thinks of us :—

"Hitherto, in common with most of my countrymen as I sup-
pose, I have thought Canada, or, to speak more accurately British

America, to be a mere strip lying north of the United States, easily detachable from the parent State, but incapable of sustaining itself, and therefore ultimately, nay right soon, to be 'taken on' by the Federal Union, without materially changing or affecting its own condition or development. I have dropped the opinion as a national conceit. I see in British North America, stretching as it does across the Continent from the shores of Labrador and Newfoundland to the Pacific, and occupying a considerable belt of the temperate zone, traversed equally with the United States by the Lakes, and enjoying the magnificent shores of the St. Lawrence with its thousands of islands in the River and Gulf, a region grand enough for the seat of a great empire."

And again, hear the words of a Colonist who has done somewhat to make his country known.

In reflecting on the future of these Provinces, the old Judge in the Colony—the redoubtable Sam Slick—tersely put on record his views when he asked, "Have you ever thought of setting them up in business on their own account, or of taking them into partnership with yourself? In the course of nature they must form some connexion soon. Shall they seek it with you, the States, or intermarry among themselves and begin the world on their own hook? These are important questions, and they must be answered soon. . . . . Things can't and won't remain long as they are. England has three things to choose for her North American Colonies. 1st, Incorporation with herself and representation in Parliament; 2nd, Independence; and 3dly, Annexation with the States." So said Judge Haliburton, and, true to his Colonial feelings, he has been in Britain agitating on behalf of the Colonies, and urging their being made an integral portion of the British Empire. But another authority of real weight also maturely considered this subject, and, in his celebrated Report, Lord Durham ably argued the question of Union of the Provinces, and declared that "Such a union would enable all the Provinces to co-operate for common purposes; and above all, it would form a great and powerful people, possessing the means of securing good and responsible government for itself, and which, under the protection of the British Empire, might in some measure counterbalance the preponderant and increasing influence of the United States in the American continent. . . . . If we wish to prevent the extension of this influence, it can only be done by raising up to the North American Colonist some nationality of his own, by elevating these small and unimportant communities into a society having some objects of national importance, and by thus giving these inhabitants a country which they will be unwilling to see absorbed into that of their powerful neighbour."

Already I am glad to say this instinct of nationality has been aroused,—already our people

feel a patriotic pride in the growth of our infant
country. It would be a wise policy to cherish and
foster this feeling, to enlarge its bounds, to promote inter-colonial trade and other intercourse,
to develope commerce and manufactures, and to
give free scope to those enterprises which will
have a tendency to advance these objects.

It is not my purpose to enter, as I have
said, upon vexed political questions, and I shall
not here ask whether a Federative or a Legis-
lative Union of the Provinces be the most desirable. Nor shall I speculate as to whether the
great North-west Territory will be eventually
annexed to Canada, which would then be ex-
tended to the head-waters of the Saskatchewan,
in the Rocky Mountains ; or whether two important British Provinces, component parts of the
General Confederation, are yet in the future in
that great country : the one having the Red River
Settlement as its governmental seat, reaching
from Canada to the Rocky Mountains, having
a breadth of about 500 miles, and embracing the
whole of the Saskatchewan Valley; and the other
comprehending Vancouver's Island, which has
been well styled the future England of the North
Pacific, and the Pacific slope. Time, in the course
of events, will develop the result in due season.
But while thus purposely refraining from such

speculations, and not wishing moreover to discuss
matters of mere local importance, there are yet
some topics under public view which claim attention, and which cannot be overlooked.

RAILWAYS AND OTHER MATERIAL PROJECTS.

We have now a Grand Trunk Railway, and
the prospects of its traffic are brightening; but
though it has linked the West with the East, and
is about—by means of that world's wonder the
Victoria Bridge, and its auxiliary branch to
Portland—to afford to Canada unbroken connection with a winter Atlantic port, it is destined
to yet further extension. Already we have this
Provincial Railway extending from Stratford,
above Toronto, to St. Thomas, below Quebec;
but it is designed to be prolonged westward to
Sarnia, on Lake Huron, and eastward to Trois
Pistoles, 100 miles from the New Brunswick
frontier. The works on the section between
St. Thomas and Rivière du Loup are being urged
on with vigour. Nova Scotia and New Brunswick, too, are each extending their iron arms
to meet the Canadian chain of railway. A line
of railway is in progress, under the control of
Nova Scotia, designed to extend from Halifax
to the New Brunswick frontier, and thence New
Brunswick purposes to continue it to St.

John, the commercial capital of New Brunswick,
—a distance of 255 miles from the Atlantic terminus at Halifax. The American interests, ever
awake, are labouring to connect this line with
Portland and Maine; but a branch is intended to
connect the "European and North American
Railway" with Miramichi, distant from Rivière
du Loup but 200 miles.

As the result, then, of these efforts in the
Lower Provinces and in Canada, I look for the
eventual extension of a main Provincial artery,
reaching from Lake Huron to the Atlantic at
Halifax; part of it constructed, it may be, as an
inter-provincial route. But I look further, and
believe that a line of railway will yet pass up the
Ottawa Valley, and present, through British territory, a highway to the Pacific. And hear what
a high American authority, quoted by Judge
Haliburton, says of this same British American
Pacific route:—

"The route through British America is in some respects preferable to that through our own territory. By the former, the
distance from Europe to Asia is some thousand miles shorter than
by the latter. Passing close to Lake Superior, traversing the
watershed which divides the streams flowing towards the Arctic
Sea from those which have their exits southward, and crossing the
Rocky Mountains, at an elevation of some 3000 feet less than at
the South Pass, the road could be here constructed with comparative cheapness, and would open up a region abounding in valuable timber and in other natural products, and admirably suited to

the growth of grain and to grazing. Having its Atlantic seaport at Halifax and its Pacific depot near Vancouver's Island, it would inevitably draw to it the commerce of Europe, Asia, and the United States. Thus British America, from a mere Colonial dependency, would assume a controlling rank in the world. To her other nations would be tributary; and in vain would the United States attempt to be her rival, for we could never dispute with her the possession of the Asiatic commerce, nor the power which that commerce confers."

And considering these statements from an impartial authority, let us echo the words of Haliburton : " What a glorious future does this prophetic vision of an American seer unfold? From our side of the border, echo will reverberate his prediction until prophecy shall accomplish its own fulfillment. Well may he regard this coming event as an eclipse, and contemplate with wonder its overshadowing influence on the political horizon of the Republic; well may Her Majesty consider this Empire in the West as the most splendid heritage in the world,—a heritage of flood and field, of strong arms and stout hearts,—the land of the brave and the free."

When that day comes, as come it assuredly will, the visions of McTaggart, who was denounced as a madman, and of Major Pye Smith, will be realized, and, in the words of the latter, " The rich productions of the East will be landed at the commencement of the West, to be forwarded and distributed throughout our North American Colonies, and to be delivered in thirty days at the ports of Great Britain. Then Halifax would be only ten or fifteen days distant from the north-west coast of America, whence steamers might be despatched with the mails from England for Pekin, Canton, Australia, and New Zealand. What rolling masses of treasure will be sure to travel on such a girdle-line of communication as this grand natural highway from the Atlantic to the Pacific!"

Another reason that might be urged for the superiority of a high northern latitude for this railroad, is, that it avoids the summer heat of a southern route, which threatens disease and death to the unacclimated European emigrant.

I look also yet to see the noble Ottawa made available for through navigation, and fleets of stately steamers pouring into our midst the wealth of the Western States, and meeting at Quebec and Montreal the Canadian lines of ocean steamers, whose trade will be maintained and supported by feeding-lines of propellers, laying, by way of the St. Lawrence and the Ottawa, the Western States and the Maritime Provinces under contribution. In this connection too it would be found immediately practicable to originate and sustain a line of steamers to the lower ports of the St. Lawrence, touching at Gaspé, the Magdalen Islands, and at ports in New Brunswick, Nova Scotia, and Prince Edward's Island, in connection with the ocean steamers.

Such, then, are some of the material projects which lie before us, and which time will develope into life and activity. As our lands become more densely settled, as the tide of population pours in upon us, this our country will increase in wealth, and will steadily develope its resources. Let us hope, then, that it will grow also in those higher moral, social, educational, and other features which mark the real prosperity of a people ; and while with all the vigor of a new world these noble Provinces are thus advancing, I doubt not some of us may be spared to look back upon what has yet been attained, as but a faint shadow of the greatness which lies before this New Britannia. Very lately, too, despite the shock of commercial depression, and the panic in the States, and the suspension of monied institutions there, our young country presented a proud aspect of stability and self-reliance; and during the whole shock of commercial credit elsewhere, our Canadian banks continued specie payments, and afforded the requisite accommodation to their customers. In Montreal, we have seen commercial confidence unimpared throughout, and our merchants standing firm as in other times.

Viewing, then, these Provinces in all their aspects, I firmly believe that the day will come, when, in the graphic language of a Canadian writer, Mr. Roche, who feels a patriotic interest in the progress of our country and has done it some service, —

"The Upper Provinces of the North-west and the Saskatchewan country, and the Lower Provinces of Nova Scotia, New Brunswick, and Prince Edward's Island, being joined to Canada, the whole confederated Provinces will ere long eclipse in importance all the other colonies of Great Britain put together, and become a mightier empire in the West than India has ever been in the East."

Still be this as it may, and distant as the event may prove, and even Utopian as some may deem it, I am content to record the views I entertain, resting assured that time as it passes will mature and develope the strength and power of British North America, and enable her sons to care for the interests entrusted to their keeping, and to consolidate the strength and develope the general resources of their country.

CONCLUDING THOUGHTS.

But long as has been the journey this evening, and vast the territory traversed, I trust that none of my hearers will consider the time ill spent which we have thus together devoted to the con-

sideration of the extent and importance of the
British North American Provinces; and I shall
therefore, at the risk of repetition, ask you, in the
graphic words of Judge Haliburton, "to take
your pencils and write down a few facts I will
give you, and, when you are alone meditating, *just
chew on 'em.*"

"There are," says he, " 4 millions of square miles of territory in
them, whereas all Europe has but 3 millions and some odd hundred thousands, and our almighty, everlasting United States still
less than that again. Canada alone is equal in size to Great Britain, France, and Prussia. The Maritime Provinces themselves
cover a space as large as Holland, Belgium, Greece, Portugal, and
Switzerland all put together. The imports for 1853 were between
10 and 11 millions, and the exports and ships sold included between 9 and 10 millions. The increase of population in ten years
is in the States 33 per cent., in Canada 68.

"Now take these facts and see what an empire is here, surely
the best in climate, soil, mineral, and other productions in the
world, and peopled by such a race as no other country under
heaven can produce. Here, Sir, are the bundle of sticks; all
they want is to be well united."

And that they will be so united in firm and
indissoluble alliance, I have no manner of doubt.
Already the prospect is engaging the attention
of thinking men, and Canada and Acadia have
begun to stretch out their hands to each other:
the alliance of their hearts and hands will follow.
Our neighbours, too, have their eyes upon us,
and see the vision of our future distinctly defined.
It is well, then, in many points of view, that this

subject should be thus early discussed, for it will
take time to attain its successful accomplishment.
Public opinion has been rapidly maturing with
regard to it. A few years ago, the man who
ventured to declare himself in favour of such a
combination was deemed a visionary, and was in
fact in advance of his times. Now, however,
politicians, and the leaders of that other power in
the state,—a power which makes and unmakes
cabinets,—the press, are ready to adopt the pro-
posal. This is cheering ; for the more that it is
weighed, the more important in every aspect of
view will this Union appear. The mere discus-
sion of it will do good ; while the actual grap-
pling with the practical details of this great national question, will give a breadth and scope to
our politics that they now lack.

The dealing with the destinies of a future
Britannic empire, the shaping its course, the
laying its foundations broad and deep, and the
erecting thereon a noble and enduring super-
structure, are indeed duties that may well evoke
the energies of our people, and nerve the arms
and give power and enthusiasm to the aspirations
of all true patriots. The very magnitude of the interests involved, will, I doubt not, elevate many
amongst us above the demands of mere sec-
tionalism, and enable them to evince sufficient

comprehensiveness of mind to deal in the spi-rit of real statesmen with issues so momentous, and to originate and develope a national line of commercial and general policy, such as will prove adapted to the wants and exigencies of our position.

But having thus directed your attention to matters that concern you all very closely, I shall only add, that, while we are thus together conjecturing as to the future of this New Britannia, this rising power on the American Continent, I cannot refrain from a passing allusion to the paramount necessity of the right developement and formation of the national character of this infant people. Nations, like individuals, have their peculiar characteristics. The British people, so firmly combined and yet so singularly distinct, present in proud pre-eminence a high-toned national character, a fit model for our imitation. Inheriting, as we do, all the characteristics of the British people, combining therewith the chivalrous feeling and the impulsiveness of France, and fusing other nationalities which mingle here with these, into one, as I trust, harmonious whole,—rendered the more vigorous by our northern position, and enterprising by our situation in this vast country which owns us as its masters,—the British American people have duties and responsibilities of no light character imposed upon them by Providence. Enjoying self-government in political matters, —bringing home, through the municipal system, the art of government, and consequent respect for it, to the whole people,—let a high ensample of national character be kept steadily in view, and let every effort be directed by our statesmen and by our whole people to its formation. A wide-spread dissemination of a sound education,—a steady maintenance of civil and religious liberty, and of freedom of speech and thought, in the possession and enjoyment of all classes of the community,—a becoming national respect and reverence for the behests of the Great Ruler of events and the teachings of his Word,—truthfulness and a high-toned commercial honour,—unswerving and unfaltering rectitude as a people, in the strict observance of all the liabilities of the Province towards its creditors, and in all its relations towards all connected with it,—a becoming respect for the powers that be, and a large and liberal appreciation of the plain and evident responsibilities of our position,—should be pre-eminent characteristics of the British American people; and so acting, they will not fail to win the respect, as they will command the notice, of the world.

But in all this do not think that you have no share; for in the formation of that character there is none so humble that he has not a part to play. Society is a complex whole: all its members are so fitly combined,—each so acts and reacts on the other,—circles of influence are ever so meeting, contending, and extending, that thus the whole derives its characters from the natures and features of its component parts. In this view, then, each individual among us is exercising an influence, more or less widely diffused, upon the society in which we mingle. And a people is, after all, but an aggregation of individual influences. Let each, then, adopt and firmly act up to high views of the social, moral, and religious duties we owe to ourselves and to society, and so the well-being of the whole will be promoted.

And to those young British Americans who are within my hearing, I would say: Be no loiterers or laggards by the way. Here, you have a princely heritage before you. Here, steady industry and unflinching integrity will secure the rise of any man. Here, there is no keen competition, no overwrought crowding of the masses; but there is the widest scope for the exercise of every species of calling. And be your position what it may, recollect that your own

conduct can dignify and elevate it. You live in
a country before which there lies a dazzlingly brilliant future : be equal to the emergencies of your
position, and recollect that you will have some
greater or smaller influence in the shaping of its
destinies. Be true, then, to yourselves, and you
cannot help rising with your country. Take a
deeper interest in its affairs, watch the course of
events, and be ready to adopt an intelligent
opinion on the requirements of daily occurrences.
Cherish and promote by all means the spread of
a national sentiment. Familiarise yourself with
all the interests of your country ; *and henceforth
feel, if you have never felt before, that you have
a country of which any people might well be
proud.*

And now, in conclusion, if anything that I
have urged will cause the pure flame of patriot-
ism to burn more brightly in the breasts of any
of my hearers, I shall feel that this endeavour
to contribute my mite towards extending somewhat more widely a knowledge of the capabilities of British North America, has been amply
rewarded.

APPENDIX.

CANADA, HER OCEAN STEAMERS, INLAND NAVIGATION, & RAILWAY SYSTEM.

* In the foregoing pages, the writer purposely dwelt less fully on matters connected with Canada than he would have done but for the reason that he was addressing a Canadian audience, who were presumed to be fully acquainted with the position of their own country. As however this pamphlet may fall into the hands of many who do not possess a similar knowledge of Canada and her resources, it has been thought advisable to supply, in this Appendix, a condensed view of the ocean and inland navigation and of the great system of railways of the Province,—features which will ensure the maintenance of that steady growth and substantial prosperty which has hitherto marked the onward course of this rising British Colony. The advance of the population has been very rapid. In 1841 that of Western Canada was 465,357. In 1851 it was 952,004, or an increase of 104 58 per cent. In 1831 the population of Lower Canada was 511,920. In 1851 it was 890,026, having doubled in twenty years. Or to view the matter in another aspect, as showing combined progress, in 1851 the population of United Canada was 1,845,265, while in 1857 it was (as ascertained by the Bureau of Agriculture and Statistics, from returns from the various municipalties) 2,571,437, showing an increase in five years of 729,172.

This noble British Province, with a healthy climate, vast resour-

* The writer acknowledges the friendly assistance and valuable suggestions, which, in the progress of this Lecture through the press, he has received from the President of the Mercantile Library Association.

ces, and ample room for the industry of a population of many
millions, is now brought within 10 or 11 days' easy sail of Britain
by the vessels of the Montreal Ocean Steamship Company, under
contract with the Canadian Government for the transport of the
mails. The line is composed of four vessels, of about 2000 tons
each ; and four others are in course of construction. They leave
Liverpool for Quebec and Montreal every second Wednesday
during the summer months, commencing 21st April, and Quebec
for Liverpool every second Saturday, commencing 22nd May.
After the present year the line will make weekly trips. In
winter their American terminus is Portland. The cabin
passage from Liverpool to Quebec is from £15 15s. to £18
18s. sterling, according to accommodation ; steerage, £8 8s.
stg., children in proportion. Freight to Montreal is 60s. stg.
per ton measurement; heavy goods as per agreement. Westward, from Liverpool to Quebec, the average passage of the Canadian line of steamers for 1857 was eleven days and one hour, being thirty-eight hours per trip better than the Cunard line to New
York, fifty-six hours better than the Collins line to New York,
and thirty-six hours better than the Cunard line to Boston.
Eastward, from Quebec to Liverpool, the average passage for 1857
was ten days and fifteen hours, being six hours per trip better than
the Cunard line from New York, thirty hours better than the
Collins line from New York, and sixteen hours better than the
Cunard line from Boston.

The difference in time is in part to be accounted for by the shorter distance of the voyage. From Liverpool to New York it is
2980 miles, and to Boston 2823 ; while to Quebec it is only 2583
miles. Besides, it must be borne in mind, that steamers passing
by way of the Straits of Belle Isle are only for about 1878 miles
upon the rough Atlantic, and have the comparatively smooth,
pleasant water of the Gulf and the River St. Lawrence for the
remainder of the passage.

Montreal, on the River St. Lawrence, 180 miles above Quebec,
is the destination or great landing-port of the ocean steamers,
where they meet steamers and other craft of from one to four
hundred tons burthen, fitted for the inland navigation of nearly

thirteen hundred miles farther west to Chicago, southwesterly
into the very centre of the North American Continent, embracing
an extent of inland water communication which is almost un-
equalled in the world, and subject to still further extension by
passing through the Sault Ste. Marie Canal into Lake Superior.
Montreal, at the head of ocean navigation, is the port of this great
inland chain, of which the St. Lawrence (westward from that
city) makes 170 miles, Lake Ontario 190, Lake Erie 250, Lake
St. Clair 25, Lake Huron 270, Lake Michigan 320, and Lake
Superior 420 miles.

This stupendous course of navigation is perfected by seven
canals, in all measuring 45 miles in length of excavation, to avoid
the rapids of the St. Lawrence. These, with their locks, are in
size and manner of construction superior to anything of the kind
known in the world; the locks being of solid heavy masonry, 9 to
feet in length, from 45 to 55 feet in width, and 10 feet deep on
the sills. Lake Ontario is connected with Lake Erie by the Welland Canal, 28 miles in length.

By the St. Lawrence and the Welland Canals passage is
afforded from the Western Lakes to the Atlantic for vessels
drawing ten feet of water and suited to the capacity of the locks.
Sailing-vessels and steamers leave Montreal daily in the summer
months for the West, and avail themselves of the St. Lawrence
Canals to avoid the rapids of that river, as also do heavily laden
vessels tending eastward; but the mail steamers from Kingston,
freighted with passengers, regularly run down all the rapids
with ease, expedition, and safety. In the summer months, there
is thus an uninterrupted water communication from the tide-
waters of the Atlantic Ocean at Quebec (the only port on the
western shores of the Atlantic north of Charleston, it may be
remarked, with the exception of Portland, where the " Leviathan "
could ride in safety and in stately grandeur) to the centre of the
American continent.

Throughout the summer months, this communication is sup-
plemented, and in winter is wholly supplied and maintained, by
the Grand Trunk Railway, commencing at St. Thomas, below
Quebec, and extending to Stratford, in Upper Canada, in one

line of 656 miles, which is unbroken except by crossing the
St. Lawrence at Montreal. But the St. Lawrence will shortly
be spanned by the Victoria Bridge, now in rapid course of
construction. This great bridge, which may be considered the
eighth wonder of the world, will be constructed at a cost of
nearly a million and a half pounds sterling. Its length will be
within fifty yards of two English miles. It will be built on 24
piers—all the spans being 240 feet, except the centre one, which
will be 330 feet and be 60 feet above high water—and on two
long abutments. The quantity of stone in these piers and abutments will amount to 250,000 tons. The piers will be traversed
by iron tubes similar to those of the Menai Bridge, which wil
contain 8000 tons of iron.

This railway is also to be prolonged westward to Stratford from
Sarnia, and eastward to Trois Pistoles from St. Thomas, and will
then, inclusively of the existing branch from Montreal to Portland,
of 292 miles, comprise an unbroken communication of 1026
miles

The running time by the Grand Trunk Railway from Quebec,
the first landing-point of the ocean steamers, to Montreal, is 8
hours; from Montreal to Ottawa City 7 hours, to Toronto 14
hours, and to Chicago 40 hours.

Fare by rail from Quebec to Montreal, 1st class $3, 2nd class
$2; Montreal to Toronto, 1st class $10, 2nd class $8; Montreal
to Ottawa, 1st class $5, 2nd class $3.50; Montreal to Chicago, 1st
class $25, 2nd class $14. Passengers are ticketed through from
Britain to Canada, or to the Western States, by the Canadian
steamers and the Grand Trunk Railway.

The Ottawa navigation at the City of Ottawa is connected with
Lake Ontario at Kingston by the Rideau Canal, constructed by
the Imperial Government at a cost of £965,000.

A canal has been commenced at Lake Chats on the Ottawa;
and a survey has been made with a view to rendering the Upper
Ottawa River available for navigation, and thus affording another
outlet to the products of the Great West. It is believed to be
quite practicable to open up by this route a river and canal navigation from Montreal to the Georgian Bay of Lake Huron,—

a route, too, to the Far West which would be 700 miles shorter than that round the Peninsula of Upper Canada.

Aided by several canals, the lower portion of the River Ottawa is navigated by steamboats to the City of Ottawa; and thence, with three short interruptions, to Les Joachims, 45 miles above Pembroke and about 265 miles from Montreal. A railroad to Prescott connects the City of Ottawa, 120 miles from Montreal, with the Grand Trunk Railway.

Canada is intersected by a number of railways, established or in course of construction, by which all parts of the Province are or will shortly be opened out. At present, winter communication is secured to the ocean by a branch of the Grand Trunk Railway running from Longueuil (opposite Montreal) to Portland, State of Maine, 292 miles from Montreal, to which the Canadian line of steamers runs from November to April. The Quebec branch of the Grand Trunk Railway joins at Richmond (70 miles from Montreal) the branch just named.

At no distant time the British North American Provinces will be connected by one grand inter-provincial railroad running from Halifax, Nova Scotia, through New Brunswick, till it joins the Canadian Grand Trunk Railway at Trois Pistoles, and connects at Montreal with the Victoria Bridge. The day too will come when a grand national chain of railway will thence pass on through British America and link the Atlantic with the Pacific.

More than three thousand miles of Canadian telegraph lines centre at Montreal, and afford communication with all parts of the continent; and should the attempt prove successful to span the broad Atlantic, and connect Britain and British America and thence the United States, with the ocean telegraph, Canadian energy has already conceived the project of imitating the example and laying down by way of the Gulf of St. Lawrence, and so across the ocean to Britain, one of those magic wires of instantaneous intelligence, which will link in unison the throbbings of the hearts of Britain and of Canada.

WORKS CONSULTED OR QUOTED FROM.

Andrews's Report on the Colonial
   and Lake Trade.
Haliburton's History of Nova Scotia.
Gesner on New Brunswick.
Monro on the Lower Provinces.
Bonnycastle's New Brunswick.
Ryerson on Hudson's Bay.

Hobbs's Hudson's Bay.
Fitzgerald on ditto.
Simpson's Overland Journey.
Bond's Minnesota.
Nicolay on British Oregon.
Howe's Speech on Nova Scotia.